5.49

5/16

TIME MACHINE MAGAZINE

Time Machine Magazine books are published by Stone Arch Books
A Capstone Imprint
1710 Roe Crest Drive
North Mankato, Minnesota 56003
www.mycapstone.com

Library of Congress Cataloging-in-Publication Data
Terrell, Brandon, 1978- author.
Pluck and perfection / by Brandon Terrell.
Summary: After a fall during her balance beam routine thirteen-year-old Rachel
and her cousin use the magical Sports Illustrated magazines in their grandfather's
collection to travel back to the 1976 Olympics to observe Nadia Comaneci's perfect
routines—and incidentally meet their grandfather who is covering the Olympics as a
sports reporter.

ISBN 978-1-4965-2595-6 (library binding)
ISBN 978-1-4965-2704-2 (paperback)
ISBN 978-1-4965-2708-0 (ebook pdf)

Comaneci, Nadia, 1961- –Juvenile fiction.–Olympic Games (21st : 1976 : Montreal,
Quebec)–Juvenile fiction. I Sports illustrated–Juvenile fiction. I Time travel–
Juvenile fiction. I Artistic gymnastics–Juvenile fiction. I Cousins–Juvenile fiction. I
Grandfathers–Juvenile fiction. I Montreal (Quebec)–History–Juvenile fiction. I CYAC:
Comaneci, Nadia, 1961- –Fiction. I Olympic Games (21st : 1976 : Montreal, Quebec)–
Fiction. I Time travel–Fiction. I Gymnastics–Fiction. I Cousins–Fiction. I Grandfathers–
Fiction. I Montreal (Quebec)–History–20th century–Fiction. I Canada–History–20th
century–Fiction.
LCC PZ7.T273 Pl 2016 I DDC 813.6–dc23

Editor: Nate LeBoutillier
Designer: Ted Williams
Illustrator: Nur Iman

Photo Credits: Sports Illustrated: Tony Triolo, 124
Design Elements: Shutterstock

Printed in the United States of America in
North Mankato, Minnesota
102015   009221CGS16

TIME MACHINE MAGAZINE

PLUCK AND PERFECTION

BY BRANDON TERRELL

STONE ARCH BOOKS
a capstone imprint

"*I don't run away from a challenge because I am afraid. Instead, I run toward it because the only way to escape fear is to trample it beneath your feet.*"

— Nadia Comaneci

CHAPTER 1

Rachel Young was cool under pressure. She always thought things through and kept a level head in every aspect of her life.

So it made absolutely zero sense that she was feeling so nervous.

It wasn't like the gymnastics competition going on outside the locker room—where she was seated on a metal bench with her head in her hands—was the state championship or anything. It was just another meet on just another Saturday. But it was the first meet that thirteen-year-old Rachel would be competing in for her new school. Her nerves were getting the best of her.

From the locker room, she heard claps and whistles from the crowd that filled the gym at Wells Middle School, home of the Fighting Warriors.

"Stop psyching yourself out," she whispered to herself.

Rachel had been a gymnast ever since she was old enough to balance on a street curb . . . then a log, then a beam. Her fearlessness made her perfect for swinging on uneven bars and vaulting into the air while twisting and turning.

Rachel stood and took a deep, calming breath. Then another. And another.

It worked.

At least, until she opened the door of the locker room and stepped out.

"Rachel!" said her cousin, Nate. "You're almost up. What took you so long?"

Nate was the same age as Rachel, but where Rachel was angular and graceful, her cousin always appeared a bit uncomfortable. He leaned against the cement wall of the corridor leading from the locker room to the gymnasium.

Rachel's recently settled nerves ran amok again.

"There's just one more competitor on the beam before you," Nate said, approaching her while reading from the folded printout of the meet's program. "Linnea Volk from Barriston Middle School. She's a really good—" Suddenly, his face contorted, and he unleashed a large sneeze, barely able to get his hand up in time to block it.

"You're not getting sick, are you?" Rachel asked.

Nate shrugged, sniffled. "Uh . . . no?"

"Ugh." She pushed him away carefully with one arm. "Keep your germs away from me."

The two cousins began to walk through the hallway and toward the gymnasium. They passed other competitors. Some spoke to one another while others mentally practiced their moves before their performance. A girl wearing a blue Morris Middle School leotard sat on the floor with her back against the wall. She was clutching her left ankle and sobbing. Another Morris gymnast knelt beside her. "It's okay, Heidi," she said reassuringly. "Let's find Coach and get you some ice."

The gym was not huge, but as Rachel stepped out onto the floor, it felt like she was standing in a large arena. The wooden bleachers were packed with people. Eight teams were competing in the meet, which meant eight collections of parents, extended families, friends, and classmates were watching and cheering. Speaking of family, Rachel spied her mom off to one side, sitting next to her grandpa. Nate's parents sat with them.

They all waved when Rachel looked up at them. She didn't want to wave back, but Nate nudged her. "Check it out," he said, elbowing her in the side. "Even Grandpa Sam came to cheer you on." Rachel lifted a hand and waved politely.

The gym was separated into sections, with each gymnastic apparatus taking up its own space. Closest to them was the vault, with its long runway and thick landing mat. Beside that was the large, thin square mat for the floor exercise. The uneven bars and beam were on the opposite side of those, near the judging tables.

"Look," Nate said. "Linnea's up on the beam."

A tall, lean figure was perched atop the balance beam. Her back was arched, and her arms were pointed toward the ceiling. She looked at ease, and even from a distance, Rachel could see a smile on her face.

The butterflies that seemed to have taken up permanent residence in her stomach fluttered around again.

"Come on," Rachel grumbled, and the two began to walk around the gymnasium.

A young blond girl with pigtails and a spring in her step was practicing her spins as they passed the floor exercise area. She swung her arms up to place them over her head—

—and struck Nate right in the chin.

His teeth clacked together.

"Oh gosh!" the young girl said. "I'm so sorry!"

Nate stumbled back a step, nearly tripping over another gymnast seated behind him on the mat, stretching. "It's . . . it's okay," Nate said. "My fault, really."

The girl went back to practicing her moves.

The rest of the Wells Middle School team— those who weren't preparing to compete—were huddled together near the beam. Coach Stephens, a tall brunette woman in black athletic pants and a blue and yellow Warriors T-shirt, stood alongside them. When Nate and Rachel reached them, Nate whispered, "Good luck," before slipping back over to the bleachers. Rachel joined her team and watched Linnea Volk.

"Man, she's good," said Norah Frederick, one of Rachel's teammates. Norah was stout and muscular, the kind of girl who could quickly and effortlessly twist around in mid-air.

As Rachel watched, Linnea completed a near-perfect pivot turn, followed by a series of cartwheels that took her to the end of the beam, finishing in lunge position. She paused, her eyes narrowing as she prepared to dismount. Friends and teammates cheered her on from the stands. Shouts of "Come on, Linnea!" and "You got this!" filled the gym.

In a flurry of motion, Linnea went straight into a pair of back handsprings. She leaped into the air, turned her body, and *whoomp!*

Her feet, stuck together perfectly, hit the mat. They didn't move an inch.

"Wow!" muttered Kelsey Parker, another of Rachel's teammates.

Thunderous applause filled the gymnasium. Linnea's grin went from ear to ear as she bounded off the mat and breezed past Rachel without a word.

Rachel's stomach did its own tumbling floor routine. *How am I supposed to follow that?* she thought. She didn't have time to answer the question, because Coach Stephens placed a hand on her shoulder and said, "Rachel, you're up."

Rachel nodded. She walked onto the mat and up to the beam, trying her hardest to clear her mind, to forget about the crowd and the scores of eyes staring her down, to forget about Linnea Volk and what was bound to be her winning routine.

As Rachel placed a hand on the beam, music began to fill the gym. The pig-tailed competitor who'd smacked Nate in the face was beginning her floor exercise. The tinny tune being piped through the gym's old speakers was grating.

"Can't let it distract me," Rachel told herself. She lifted her chin and raised her hands to the sky to signify the start of her routine. Applause rang from the crowd as she placed her hands on the beam, leaped up with her legs apart, and straddled the beam.

Over the sound of the floor routine music, Rachel heard Norah shout, "You can do it, Rachel!"

Rachel began her routine with dance elements, walking forward and back, swooping her arms around in graceful motions. She took a lunge step, dropping to one knee, then to her backside, where she rolled backward into a handstand.

Applause rang out in the gym.

Keep your focus, Rachel thought. She was in the zone now. All worry and fear about her performance washed away.

Until she was back on her feet executing a pirouette.

It was just a simple turn, one she'd done countless times. But when she turned, her left foot faltered, and she started to lose her balance. It wasn't a major deduction, but it ripped her out of the zone and stomped on her focus.

She forged ahead, leaping into the air and doing a scissors leap. When her feet hit the beam, a cloud of chalk puffed out around them.

From there, Rachel walked to the end of the beam. She spun, stepped, and flipped into a forward handspring. Her momentum was too much, though, and when her front foot landed on the beam, her ankle twisted. Rachel's arms flailed up, like she was struggling to stay above water, pinwheeling. Her right foot struck her left, and before she knew what was happening, Rachel toppled backward off the beam.

She hit the mat hard. The wind expelled from her lungs. She heard the crowd gasp, but was too stunned to move, lying on her back and staring up at the criss-crossing beams of the gymnasium ceiling high above. She tried to suck in air, but couldn't. Instead, a choking cough escaped her lips.

The world around her had gone quiet. Even the stupid floor exercise music had faded out. The gym was a massive, hollow room.

Get up! she urged herself. *Get up and finish your routine!*

But she couldn't. The fall had been too much. She could move her body—it wasn't like she was injured or anything—but the embarrassment and shame flooding through her was enough to keep her pinned to the mat. She'd never fallen in a competition before. Never like this.

Coach Stephens was beside her then, kneeling down, eyebrows furrowed. "Are you hurt?" she asked.

Rachel shook her head. "Just my pride," she muttered, brushing Coach Stephens aside and standing on her own.

The crowd must have thought she'd been injured. They broke into a solemn round of applause as she stood. Rachel was keenly aware of everyone's eyes on her. Coach Stephens backed away, and Rachel lined up to mount the beam again.

As she pulled herself up, though, she felt a wave of paralyzing fear wash over her. It was something she'd never experienced before. It made her hands shake and the hair on the back of her neck stand. She wobbled and then righted herself. It was almost like she could feel the crowd take and hold a collective breath.

She looked down at her feet. Suddenly the four-inch-wide beam shrank. The four feet from the beam to the mat grew. Rachel felt like a high-wire artist perched in the sky, one misstep from tumbling to her death.

I can't do this, she thought. And though she tried to brush the words away, they repeated in her head like tiny punches to the stomach. *I can't do this. I can't do this. I can't do—*

Rachel leaped down off the beam. Murmurs of confusion spread across the gym as she began to walk off the mat and past her teammates.

"Rachel?" Nate asked as she passed him. "What's wrong?"

She didn't answer.

Hot tears stung the corners of her eyes. She didn't want to wipe them away, didn't want people to see that she was crying. When she looked up and saw her grandpa and mom staring back at her, though, it was too much.

Rachel clamped a hand to her mouth, broke into a run, and fled the gymnasium for the comforting emptiness of the locker room.

"The filing cabinet," she whispered, surprised by the loudness of her voice in the silent space.

One of Grandpa Sam's most prized possessions was a filing cabinet filled with magazines. A few were loose, their pages ancient and brittle, but most were packaged in plastic bags for protection. Almost all of them were issues of *Sports Illustrated*.

The magazines contained more than articles and photos. They contained magic. At any time, an issue of *Sports Illustrated*—the right issue—could send Rachel and her cousin back in time.

The blue spark of electricity came from atop the cabinet. Rachel wove through the basement to the cabinet to see what adventure awaited her.

The magazine was in mint condition, concealed in a plastic bag with a thin white board behind it to keep it from bending. In the moonlight, Rachel saw the magazine's cover. On it was a photo of a young, smiling girl confidently thrusting both arms into the air. The girl was about Rachel's

age, maybe younger. She wore a long-sleeved, white leotard, and her brown hair hung evenly across her forehead. *SHE STOLE THE SHOW*, the magazine read in bold yellow letters. And below it was a name.

"Nadia Comaneci," Rachel whispered.

She cranked her head and looked around suspiciously. First left, then right. She fully expected Grandpa Sam to be standing behind her. He was not.

As her eyes scanned the basement, she caught a glimpse of a similar photo of the gymnast. This one was in black and white, and was part of a news article. In the blue sliver of moonlight cast along the wall, she read the headline aloud. "The Darling of Montreal." Below the headline were the words: *By Sam Winstead*.

She knew the article, knew the headline. Grandpa Sam talked about it often, whenever they sat in the peace and quiet of Clear Lake and enjoyed a leisurely afternoon. "That article," he'd tell them, "got me a promotion that gave your grandmother and I enough money to buy this place. Best story I ever wrote. Seeing that young lady compete at the Olympics was one of the highlights of my career."

Rachel turned her attention back to the *Sports Illustrated* on the cabinet. As she reached for the magazine, a small jolt of energy pulsed in her fingers. It trailed up her hand, wrist, and arm. She watched the strands of energy and how they connected her to the magazine. But she wasn't worried about unleashing its power. Not yet. In order for the *Sports Illustrated* to send her back in time, she knew she needed to read the cover article. And though she couldn't be sure, Rachel thought she also needed something else to time travel.

Or rather, some*one* else.

"Nate," she said quietly.

Above her, the floor creaked. Rachel gasped. *Someone else is awake!*

Abandoning the magazine, she scurried back up the stairs and into the kitchen just before her mom, bleary-eyed and nearly sleepwalking, entered.

"Hey," her mom said with a scratchy voice. She rubbed her eyes. "Saw the light on. Everything okay?"

Rachel tried to get her heart to stop pounding in her chest. She nodded. "Couldn't sleep," she said.

Her mom screwed her face up into a look of understanding. "Don't worry so much," she said. "You're a fantastic gymnast. You'll feel much better in the morning, so try to get some sleep, okay?"

"Okay." Rachel set her empty water glass in the sink and followed her mom out of the kitchen. She clicked the light off after her.

As she slipped back under the covers, her mind was no longer on the gymnastics meet. She didn't think she would be dreaming of falling anymore.

No, for the rest of the night, she would dream of time traveling.

CHAPTER 3

The following morning, Rachel waited for Nate by his locker. She stood there for almost ten minutes, constantly checking her watch. For all his success in class, Nate almost always ran behind schedule.

Finally, he showed, saying, "Oh, so now you want to talk to me?"

Rachel rolled her eyes. "Knock it off," she said. "I'm sorry, okay."

"It's fine," he said. He popped open his locker and began to shovel his gigantic textbooks out of his backpack and onto the thin metal shelf at the top of the locker. "I just don't get why it's such a big deal. So you fell. You get up. You try again. Nobody's perfect."

"Easy for you to say," Rachel replied under her breath.

"What's so important that you're gonna make me late for Algebra class?" Nate asked. He wiped his nose with a tissue and then shoved it into the pouch of his sweatshirt pouch where other crumpled tissues poked out.

"I saw one of the magazines last night," she said, lowering her voice so no one could hear. Even if someone *was* eavesdropping, they'd have no clue what the cousins were discussing. Or they'd think Nate and Rachel were crazy.

Nate's interest picked up. "Like, one of Grandpa Sam's *SI*s?"

"No, a copy of *World's Dumbest Cousins*," Rachel said sarcastically. "Yeah, a *Sports Illustrated*."

"What was on the cover?"

"A photo of Nadia Comaneci at the 1976 Summer Olympics."

Nate mulled this over. "She was a gymnast, right?"

"Yeah. She recorded the first perfect score in Olympic history. A perfect ten."

"Whoa."

"She actually got seven of them."

"Seven?"

"Yeah. That means her score started at ten," Rachel explained, "and she wasn't deducted at all. That's crazy impossible. They've changed the rules since, making it a more complicated, but fair system."

"What about your team? Can you get a perfect ten?"

Rachel shrugged. "We start with a score of zero, and accumulate points with our different elements."

Nate shook his head. "Seven perfect scores."

"Yeah. And I think we're supposed to go see her do it."

Nate's eyes grew wide. "Now?"

"Does it look like I have the magazine on me?"

"Oh. Right."

"My mom woke up and I panicked. Ran back upstairs before I could get it. Tonight, though. I'll bring the magazine over after everyone goes to sleep."

Nate slammed his locker closed as the first bell rang through the halls of Wells Middle School. "Tonight," he said.

He held out his hand for Rachel to high-five. As she slapped it, she remembered the tissues in his pocket. "Gross," she said.

The second bell filled the school's halls, followed by the shuffle of tardy students rushing off to class. Rachel hurried off to the nearest bathroom to scrub her germ-covered hand.

It was nearing midnight when Rachel chucked a pebble at Nate's second-story bedroom window. She'd walked the two miles from the cabin at Clear Lake into the town of Wells, staying in the shadows and avoiding cars that passed on the road.

The stone plinked softly off the glass and then fell back to the ground. She waited a minute, hidden in the shadows of the oak tree in the Winsteads' front yard with the hood of her coat pulled up and her backpack slung across one shoulder.

No light.

She tried again, finding a slightly larger pebble and throwing it harder at the window. *Clack!*

Nothing.

Did he forget and fall asleep?

Rachel had been patient enough to wait up until her mom and grandpa both went to sleep before sneaking down to the basement to find— thankfully!—that the magazine was still there. But now she was growing impatient.

She found a third stone, the largest one yet. She aimed for Nate's window and sent it flying just as he appeared and slid the window up. The rock connected solidly with his forehead.

"Ow!" he hissed.

"Sorry!" Rachel whispered up to him. "Let me in."

"Patio," he said, rubbing his forehead. Then he disappeared.

She slunk around to the backyard, through a set of shrubs and onto the patio. A moment later, Nate slid open the large glass door leading into the house.

Without a word, they made their way back up to Nate's bedroom. When the door had been shut and they were safe, Rachel pulled off her hood and asked, "What took you so long?"

"I fell asleep studying." He pointed to his desk, where a yellow glow from a lamp lit a large history textbook and Nate's notes. Next to it was a half-empty tissue box. Several crumpled-up tissues littered the desk, while even more filled the wastebasket beneath. Rachel could see a puddle of drool soaking into Nate's spiral bound notebook.

"Gross," she said.

"Let's see it." Nate was holding out a hand, waiting for her to pass over the *Sports Illustrated*.

"Yeah, maybe I should just hold it," she said, unzipping the backpack and taking out the magazine. It was still in its protective bag.

"Wow," Nate said, marveling at the cover and condition of the magazine. "It's like it's never been read before."

"Yeah," Rachel said. "I hate the idea of taking it out." But in order for the magic to work, she needed to read from the article about Nadia Comaneci. So with shaking fingers, she split the two strips of clear Scotch tape on the back of the plastic bag. Then she opened the flap and removed the magazine.

The energy released by the *Sports Illustrated* was more intense now, like the plastic had dulled the sensation. Rachel looked over at Nate. "You ready?"

"As ready as I'll ever be, I guess."

Rachel nodded at the thick textbook on his desk. "Time to stop studying history and start living it."

"How long have you been waiting to say *that* one?" Nate asked with a straight face.

She shrugged. "Just thought of it," she said.

"Sure." He didn't sound like he believed her.

Rachel flipped open the *Sports Illustrated* and found the article about Nadia Comaneci. She began to read. "*There are so many athletes at the Olympics, and so many winners, but in the first week there was only one star, a child named Nadia Comaneci.*"

Blue light began to flicker and roil from the magazine's pages. Rachel had to stop herself from dropping it.

"The heightened security is a direct response to the horrors of Munich," said a voice with a thick British accent from behind. Rachel spun on a heel to see who was speaking to them.

A tall and lean boy stood before them. He had curly brown hair, a dimpled smile, and a pair of narrow glasses perched on his nose. The boy was about their age, or slightly older, and wore a grey sports coat and a pair of khaki pants. He held a large brown briefcase.

The boy smiled. "Apologies for frightening you," he said. "It certainly was not my intent." He held out a hand. "Nigel Bellflower."

Rachel's heart fluttered like a hummingbird. Then she reached out and shook his hand. It was warm and inviting. "Rach—Uh, Natalie Smith," she said. "This is my cousin . . . Richard."

Nate gave her a confused look. "Hey," he said.

Nigel set his oversized briefcase on the cement sidewalk and reached out to shake Nate's hand. Thinking fast, Rachel swatted it away.

45

"Excuse me?" a confused Nigel asked.

"Sorry," Rachel said. "He's sick. What were you saying about Munich?"

"The increased security." Nigel nodded in the direction of a passing police officer. "All an effort to make sure the terrorist situation at the previous Games in Munich, Germany, is not repeated."

Rachel briefly remembered reading about the hostage situation in her history book. Or maybe she had watched a movie about it.

"I spotted your passes," Nigel said, breaking her train of thought and producing a similar *Junior Press* pass from inside his coat. "The rest of the young journalists are meeting in five minutes to ride the bus back to our hotel. Will you join us?"

Rachel nodded. "Absolutely."

"Perfect." Nigel adjusted his glasses, flashed one more smile in Rachel's direction, and then scuttled off into the crowd.

Rachel noticed he'd forgotten the case. "Wait!" she shouted. She lifted the case up, and it was deceptively heavy. *What exactly is he carrying around?* she wondered.

Nigel walked back, looking embarrassed. "So sorry," he said, taking the case from her.

"Pretty heavy briefcase," she said, saying anything to keep speaking to the young man.

"It's my typewriter," Nigel said. He rapped on the plastic case with his knuckles. "My trusty, most-prized possession."

Rachel smiled. "Cool."

"Cool?" Nigel looked baffled.

"I mean . . . it's, well, I haven't seen anyone use a typewriter in a long time."

"You haven't?"

"Never mind." Rachel realized she was digging herself into a hole, and it was best to just keep her mouth shut.

"Very well," Nigel said. "Until we meet again, Natalie Smith."

"Yeah." Rachel bit her bottom lip and again watched Nigel make his way through the crowd.

"Gross," Nate said, reading her face perfectly. "Stop ogling Brit Boy. He's older than our parents."

"What?" Then she thought about it and added, "Oh. Well, in 1976 he isn't!"

"Whatever."

"Besides," Rachel said, "you almost shook his hand. With that stupid cold of yours, you're going to get somebody sick and it's going to alter the entire history of the world."

"Don't be so dramatic. I'm fine." He paused and sneezed. "Also, good call on the fake names."

"Thanks. It's best if we don't go around spouting off our real ones."

Nate continued to alternate between sneezing, coughing, and snapping photos. Rachel took in their surroundings. The world around her seemed hopeful for an ideal Summer Games.

Finally, she saw a bus sporting the familiar Montreal Olympic symbol. The bus motored to a stop by Nigel and a group of other teens.

Rachel quickly made her way through the crowd, Nate at her side. As they neared the bus, though, she sensed her cousin slowing a bit. Nigel and the others were boarding. He lugged the large briefcase containing the typewriter with him.

"Come on," she urged Nate, who'd halted.

"Hold on," Nate said, holding up a hand. His body hitched. His nose twitched. He turned his head and unleashed a whopping sneeze—right into the face of a passing stranger. "Oh, man," he said. "I'm sorry!"

The gentleman, broad-shouldered and wearing a fedora, stopped in shock. He said nothing but removed a handkerchief from his back pocket.

Rachel rushed back and grabbed Nate by the shoulders. "We're so sorry, sir," she said.

"It's all right," the man said in a gruff voice.

And then the man finished wiping his face and looked up at her for the first time. Rachel froze. The world around seemed to come to a screeching halt.

She realized that she was staring at a younger version of Grandpa Sam!

CHAPTER 5

Rachel was stunned. Horrified. *Oh, no! Nate
just blasted Grandpa Sam with snot!* She tried
her best to stay cool and to not stare at the
wrinkle-free version of her grandpa standing
right in front of her.

Nate had not yet recognized him. "Again, so
sorry, sir," he said. He reached out to help Grandpa
Sam, but the man recoiled.

"I said it was all right," their grandpa said. He
didn't seem too excited to be talking to a couple of
kids. Or that he'd been sneezed on. "Gonna be late
for my press conference now."

Rachel nudged Nate with her foot.

"What?" he asked her, annoyed.

She said nothing, but played with the press
pass around her neck and nodded in the direction
of their grandpa.

He still didn't catch on. "Sorry," he said.

"We get it. We're junior reporters ourselves.

She's the Lois Lane," he held up his camera,

"and I'm the Jimmy Olson. You know, I bet if you

hurry, you can still make your press conference,

Mr. . . . " Nate leaned in now to read the press

badge pinned to the lapel of his grandpa's blazer.

"Mr. . . . Sam Winstead."

Rachel swore that, at that very moment, she could see the tiny gerbil in Nate's brain running furiously on its wheel as his mind put the pieces together.

"Sam *Winstead*?" said Nate.

"Yes," their grandpa said. "My name. Sam Winstead." His mood changed a bit when he realized Nate had recognized the name. He flashed a smile. "You've heard of me?"

Rachel wanted to laugh and say, *Heard of you? You're our grandpa!* Instead, she just shook her head. Nate followed her lead.

Sam's mood clouded over again. "Oh. Well, got to get to that press conference, Lois and Jimmy."

And he swiftly walked away.

Rachel watched him go. "That was so weird," she said.

The two teens hurried off in the opposite direction to catch the bus before it left.

"You are not going to make me miss the opening ceremony," Rachel said. She had her hands on her hips, and was glaring down at one of the hotel room's twin-sized beds. Nate lay there with the covers pulled up to his chin and a box of tissues next to his pillow.

It was the following afternoon, and Nate had spent the night hacking and wheezing and making it hard to sleep. Thankfully, Rachel had found a pair of earplugs in the bathroom. His cold was full-blown now, so Rachel was staying as far away from him as possible.

Their hotel was near the Olympic Village, but not a part of it. The bus driver who brought the junior reporters to the hotel the day before, told them, "No media is allowed inside the Olympic Village, and no contact with athletes is permitted." He'd then deposited them outside a tall brick building, near a set of glass double doors.

Rachel feared they wouldn't have a room since she and Nate weren't exactly part of the group. Yet

54

when they spoke with the receptionist, they had a bit of good luck. A group of junior reporters from Sweden were unable to attend, so the receptionist at the hotel placed Nate and Rachel in one of the vacant rooms.

"I can't do it," Nate said from his spot in bed. "I'm too tired."

Rachel slipped her lanyard over her neck. "Fine. But the magazine wanted me to be here, so I'm going to find out why."

She walked over to the large television resting on a wooden dresser and clicked it on with a *thunk* by twisting the dial. It slowly came to life, and a slightly-blurred image of a cereal commercial began to play.

"Not exactly high-definition," Nate croaked.

"No complaining," Rachel said. "I'll be back later."

Their room was on the third floor of the hotel. Rachel saw a few other junior reporters in the hallway. The red and orange-patterned carpet they stood on must have been designed with the sole purpose of giving people migraine headaches.

In the lobby, Nigel lounged in a blue armchair. He was writing something in a pocket notebook. He looked up and smiled as she approached. "Greetings," he said, and she couldn't seem to get past his wonderful accent.

She was able to squeak out a soft, "Hi."

"Where is your photographer companion?"

"My cousin," Rachel said quickly. "Yeah, he's sick."

"That's terribly unfortunate." Nigel stood, brushed his pants smooth. "If you'd like, I'd be glad to accompany you today."

Rachel could feel the blood rush to her cheeks. "That . . . that'd be great."

They sat together near the back of the bus on the ride to the stadium. Nigel peppered her with questions, asking about her home and her friends and her family. It felt to Rachel like he was in reporter mode, interviewing her for an article. She tried to be as vague as possible with her answers. She asked a few questions back and discovered that he lived in Wales, had a younger sister, did well in school, and played cricket.

So, basically, he was completely perfect.

As they pulled up to the stadium, Nigel said, "It's so wonderful to get to know you. I'd enjoy continuing our friendship after the Games are over."

"Yeah," Rachel said, flustered. "Me too. Maybe we can be Facebook friends."

Nigel looked puzzled. "Come again?"

"Oh!" Rachel shouted as she caught her error. She pointed out the window to redirect his attention. "Look at all the people!"

Nigel turned to look out the window and the swelling crowd outside.

Idiot, Rachel scolded herself. *Facebook? Seriously? It's 1976. The guy who invented Facebook hasn't even been born yet!*

They filed from the bus out into the massive crowd. As one, the teens were directed to a separate stadium entrance used for the press. Rachel looked around on the off chance she'd see Grandpa Sam again, but no luck.

As they stepped into the stadium, Rachel was filled with awe. A red track encompassed the grassy infield, and thousands of people filled up the seats. She stared up at the blue sky high above the stadium. Columns curved upward along the length of the circular building, making the architecture appear as if it was a ribcage, and the athletes were its heart.

"Here you are," Nigel said, pointing to her seat and taking the one beside her.

Soon, the Opening Ceremony began. A giant black screen hung high in the stadium lit up with the words *JEUX DE LA XXI OLYMPIADE MONTREAL 1976*.

Shortly after, a French-speaking announcer's voice boomed from the loudspeakers, and the crowd began to applaud. An older woman in a light pink dress and hat, a white purse draped

over one arm, came out. She took her seat on a
dais on their side of the stadium.

Rachel craned her neck to see the woman.
"Who is that?" she asked.

"The Queen Mother," Nigel replied. "Queen
Elizabeth of England."

The Canadian national anthem, "Oh, Canada," began to play. The whole stadium stood.

When it was complete, the Olympic teams began to parade through the stadium, presenting their flags as they walked along. "I believe I heard that ninety-two nations are competing in these Games," Nigel said. "Alas, many African nations have boycotted for political reasons."

"That's too bad," Rachel responded. Normally, when Nate would spout off facts like that, Rachel would roll her eyes or do her best to ignore him. But Nigel? She was hooked on his every British-accented word.

When the Russian team—announced as the U.S.S.R.—walked past in peach-toned blazers and green shirts, Nigel leaned in and said, "I'm very excited to see the Soviet women's gymnastic team compete. It will be hard to beat such phenomenal athletes as Olga Korbut and Nelli Kim." He waved at the team as they passed, as if the gymnasts were his old friends.

"I don't know," Rachel countered. "I'd keep a close eye on Nadia Comaneci if I were you. She may have a trick or two up the sleeves of her leotard."

"The girl from Romania?" Nigel studied Rachel to see if she knew something he did not. Of course, she did, but she kept a stone face. "Fascinating," he said.

"Very," she said back.

"I meant you, Natalie."

Rachel was taken aback. "Me what?"

"I find *you* fascinating. Quite fascinating, in fact."

"Oh." For about the twelfth time that day, Rachel blushed.

They watched as the team from the United States walked past, the men in blue blazers, the white-shirted women carrying oversized red bags. And the home team's athletes, the Canadians, were a sea of bright red coursing along the track.

Speaking French, the Queen of England announced the start of the Games. An enormous white flag was raised, and thousands of white pigeons were released and flew in diving circles around the applauding stadium. Finally, two young athletes—a boy with a helmet of curly hair and a girl with straight brown hair—ran onto a podium with a flaming torch held high. As they touched the licking flames to a massive white saucer, the fire took, and a larger flame began to burn brightly.

The sight was so breathtaking, Rachel reached over and took Nigel's hand without thinking. He did not pull away.

The bus returned back to the hotel late that evening. Rachel parted ways with Nigel in the lobby. He bowed his head, took her hand, and lightly kissed it. "I had an enchanting time today, Natalie," he said.

"Me too," she said.

Rachel breezed up to the third floor on a cloud of air, full of light and amazement and joy over how the day went. Humming her way down the hall, with its icky carpet, toward her and Nate's room, Rachel heard a sudden burst of coughing coming from the open vending area just ahead. She slowed, somehow alarmed by the sound.

She poked her head around the corner and peered into the vending area. Next to a line of machines with soda can labels and candy bar wrappers she hardly recognized, a man was hunched over the ice machine. He was filling a plastic bucket.

He coughed again, followed by a sneeze and a sniffle. Drawing a handkerchief from his pocket, he blew his nose viciously into it.

Rachel's heart grew cold, and the perfect experience at the Opening Ceremony with Nigel was washed away.

The sneezing man was Grandpa Sam.

He wiped his nose again, then pocketed the handkerchief, and turned. His eyes were watery, and there were large bags under them.

"Oh," he said when he saw her standing in the doorway. His voice was full of gravel and phlegm. "It's you." He paused, cradled the ice bucket in his arm to brace himself, and then sneezed again.

He's sick, she thought, coming to an obvious conclusion. *But he can't be sick! He's supposed to write about Nadia Comaneci. It's one of the most important stories of his career!*

"Tell your friend thanks for the cold," he said grumpily as he brushed past her. "Because of him, I'm gonna be laid up in bed tomorrow, sleeping off whatever he gave me."

Rachel opened her mouth, tried to speak, but no words came out.

Grandpa Sam shuffled down the hall with his ice bucket in hand, coughing and sneezing the whole way. Rachel watched him trudge to the end of the hall, turn a key in his hotel room door, and slip from sight before she ran back to her room.

She slammed the door so hard when she came in that she woke Nate from a deep sleep. He leapt into the air, his legs and arms flailing, the sheets flying up into the air like a ghost.

He snorted, sneezed, and fell back onto the bed. "What's happening?"

"Wake up," Rachel said sharply.

"Hello to you, too," Nate said, turning his head on the pillow and snuggling back in. "How was the Opening Ceremony?"

Rachel had no intention of discussing it. "I just saw Grandpa getting ice down the hall," she yipped.

"He's at our hotel? Cool."

"Not cool. He's sick. Just like you. And now he's not going to go to the gymnastics competition tomorrow. He won't see Nadia Comaneci's perfect score, won't write his article, and . . . and . . ." She had to sit down on the edge of her own bed to gather her thoughts and try to calm down.

"I'm sure he'll be fine," Nate said, trying to sound hopeful but letting a bit of guilt slip into his voice.

"We changed our own history," Rachel whispered. "Grandpa's history. Who knows what will happen now?"

made her miss it terribly, but it also began to fill her with anxiety.

She closed her eyes and took a steadying breath, like she did before every event.

It seemed to help, and she focused on the floor again. The beams—even and uneven alike—stood like bookends at either side. Between them, running next to one another, were the vault and the floor exercise area, one a chaotic burst of contained power, the other a sweeping display of posture and poise.

And there, standing beside her female coach and Romanian teammates, Rachel saw Nadia Comaneci.

She wore a white leotard, and a thick, colorful ribbon in her brown hair, just like she did on the cover of *Sports Illustrated* tucked away in the backpack at Rachel's feet. A nearby camera was directed at her, a red light atop it glowing brightly. *She looks so calm*, Rachel marveled, *considering the eyes of the world will be on her soon.*

"Six gymnasts from each team will compete

today," Nigel explained. "Their scores will determine who wins the team gold."

The competition began, with an array of athletes performing across the floor. Rachel's eyes bounced from one event to the next. She was curious to soak it all in, to see what makes an Olympic athlete special, what makes them the best in the world.

In the second round of events, Nadia readied for the uneven bars.

"This is it," Rachel said, grabbing Nigel's arm and squeezing it.

At first, the crowd around them was not sure what to make of the small, spritely athlete. She stood at the edge of the mat, preparing herself before running toward the bars, leaping into the air, hitting the vault, and catapulting over the lower bar. Her legs split, and she snatched the upper bar cleanly. It bowed in the middle as she swung down, kicked her legs, and brought her body up and over.

Rachel held her breath as she watched.

CHAPTER 7

"A perfect ten," Nigel said, shaking his head, still amazed hours later. "No Olympic athlete has ever accomplished that before."

"She deserved it," Rachel said. She was seated beside Nigel on the bus. Nate sat behind them, in a seat by himself. "I've never seen anyone perform moves like that."

For the remainder of the day's competition, it seemed like all people wanted to talk about was Nadia's performance. Rachel passed a number of television reporters discussing the day's events in English and French and German and Spanish and several other languages. The only words she understood in all of the different languages?

"Nadia Comaneci." *The Darling of Montreal*.

Rachel had been so swept away by Nadia— and, to be honest, by Nigel Bellflower—that she'd momentarily forgotten her grandpa, sick and alone in a hotel bed. She turned to stare out the window, guilty that she'd taken her eyes off the real problem.

"Everything all right?" Nigel asked.

Rachel forced a nod. "Yep," she said.

They said goodbye to Nigel in the hotel lobby. As the two teens entered their hotel room, Nate flopped down face first onto his bed. "Come to me, my cozy bed!" he shouted in a muffled voice.

Rachel couldn't rest, so she went to check on Grandpa Sam. The Do Not Disturb sign still dangled from his doorknob. She knocked anyway.

As before, Grandpa Sam took an eternity to answer. "Still not so great at reading signs," he said. Then he noticed her empty hands. "What? No gifts this time?"

He wore a white terrycloth robe and matching slippers. He tightened the robe's sash and sat down in a great heap in one of the desk chairs by the window. A typewriter sat on the table, a stack of unused white paper and a black folder next to it.

A full day of rest and relaxation hadn't helped him much. He still looked disheveled and out of sorts.

Rachel stood near the door, hesitant to enter.

"Oh, come in already," he said. "I promise I won't sneeze on you."

Rachel closed the door behind her. As she stepped into the room, though, she saw something that made her heart skip a beat. An open suitcase, filled with clothes, sat next to an envelope and a plane ticket.

"Are you leaving?" she asked.

Grandpa Sam snorted. "And stay here another day feeling like this? I'm heading back to New York tomorrow morning. Found a flight out of here leaving at eight. Better to be miserable at home."

"Did you see any gymnastics events today?"

"Caught some of it. Spent a lot of time focusing on Olga and the Soviets, and not enough on that Romanian girl, if you ask me."

"She got a perfect score on the uneven bars," Rachel said. "It was amazing. You really need to stay until tomorrow. Come to the Forum to see her on the beam. She's going to do it again."

"Score another perfect ten?" He leaned forward in his chair, the reporter in him wanting to dig deeper. "How do you know this?"

Because I'm from the future! Because you're my grandpa and you've already written about it! Because I have a Sports Illustrated *with Nadia Comaneci on the cover right here in my backpack!* All things Rachel wanted to say but couldn't. She needed to restore order—needed things to fall back into line.

CHAPTER 8

Rachel had been pacing the hotel room floor for so long, she was surprised she hadn't worn grooves in the carpet yet. She held the newspaper article in her hands, reading it in bits and pieces. Most of the print was legible, though the ink was smudged in places.

The Darling of Montreal. The words echoed in her head. *The Darling of Montreal.*

"So what are you gonna do with it?" Nate asked, scooping the *Sports Illustrated* off the bed.

Rachel shook her head. "I don't know."

"Why hasn't it disappeared? I mean, if Grandpa's not gonna write the article, it should disappear. Right?"

Rachel shrugged. "Maybe it's tied to the magazine," she suggested. "Maybe once we leave—*if* we leave—it'll disappear. Or maybe . . . "

And then she saw it. Or didn't see it. Or started to not see it. The newspaper article was starting to fade. She thought maybe it was her eyes, but as she held it, the gray letters and photos began to get hazy.

"Oh, no!" she shouted.

Nate ran over and peered over her shoulder at the article. "It's vanishing!" he said.

In a matter of minutes, she would be holding in her hands a different news story altogether.

"We have to do something," Rachel said.

"But what?"

"I don't know. Let me think."

There was still time to fix the future. But she'd need to control the fear bubbling up inside her and begging to take over.

She snapped her fingers and pointed at the nightstand table between the two hotel beds. "Get me the pen and notepad," she said, rushing over to sit at the small table in the corner.

Nate hurried over and snatched the pen and paper. He brought it to her.

CHAPTER 9

Their seats for the second day of competition were better than the day before, mostly because they were sitting near the balance beam. Rachel kept her eye out for Nadia, who practiced with her teammates. The gymnast wore the same leotard as the day before, white with colored stripes along the side. None of the gymnasts spoke; they were working very hard to focus.

Grandpa Sam's words rattled around in Rachel's head. *Life ain't about perfection; it's about not letting the fear win.* She looked close at Nadia and saw the fierce determination in her eyes.

She'd spent so much time recently—the competition and the entire trip to the past—trying to make everything perfect. When she couldn't, fear began to seep through the cracks until there was enough to take over.

When Nadia's turn arrived, Rachel leaned forward in her seat. The nimble gymnast leaped onto the beam with complete grace. She posed for one second with her leg extended so her body was shaped like an 'L', then moved into a handstand.

The crowd hushed. One man nearby continued to speak and laugh; his wife hit him with her purse and shushed him like a librarian.

Following her handstand, Nadia performed a series of skips and steps, keeping both her cool and her balance. From the end of the beam, she executed a series of backflips that made Rachel's breath catch in her throat. Then came an aerial somersault, something Rachel had never done before, as well as cartwheels and a split leap into the air. It was all capped off by another spectacular handstand.

"She's going to do it again, isn't she?" Nigel asked, nudging Rachel in the arm. "She's going to get another perfect score."

TIME MACHINE MAGAZINE
VALOR AND VICTORY

BY BRANDON TERRELL

Sports Illustrated KIDS

TIME MACHINE MAGAZINE
PLUCK AND PERFECTION

BY BRANDON TERRELL

Sports Illustrated KIDS

TIME MACHINE MAGAZINE
HARMONY AND HOOPS

BY BRANDON TERRELL

Sports Illustrated KIDS

TIME MACHINE MAGAZINE
GRIT AND GOLD

BY BRANDON TERRELL

Sports Illustrated KIDS

TIME MACHINE
MAGAZINE